IZZARD

IZZARD

By Lonzo Anderson

Illustrated by Adrienne Adams

CHARLES SCRIBNER'S SONS / NEW YORK

To Jeff Hotchkiss

Text copyright © 1973 John Lonzo Anderson
Illustrations copyright © 1973 Adrienne Adams

THIS BOOK PUBLISHED SIMULTANEOUSLY IN
THE UNITED STATES OF AMERICA AND IN CANADA.
COPYRIGHT UNDER THE BERNE CONVENTION.

1 3 5 7 9 11 13 15 17 19 **RD/C** 20 18 16 14 12 10 8 6 4 2
Printed in the United States of America

Library of Congress Catalog Card Number 72-9032
SBN 684-13247-8

FOREWORD

The story takes place on the island of St. John
in the Virgin Islands, where it is warm enough
all the time for lizards to live.

I found a lizard egg, tiny and white and round. I brought it home.

I held it in my hand while I took my nap in the hammock.

Tickle-tickle.

I woke up.

Wriggle-wriggle. Something was alive in my hand.

I opened my palm. There lay two pieces of egg-shell and a tiny, shiny lizard staring at me.

"Oh, look-look-look!" I yelled.

My mother looked. "How sweet," she said. "But there are lizards all over the place. We don't need any more."

My father looked. "The heat of your hand made it hatch," he said.

My sister looked. "It's darling! Oh, please! Give it to me!"

"I will not," I said. "It's mine."

It started to walk. I was afraid it would run away.

But no. After a while it scampered up my arm. Its feet made the tiniest tickle I ever felt on my skin.

It looked up at me, right in my eyes!

It ran across my sleeve to my shoulder. Up my bare neck it came, and onto my chin.

"What can I give it to eat?" I wondered.

"Nothing," my father said. "It will know what to do when the time comes to eat."

"May I keep it?"

"You haven't much choice," my father said. "It thinks you are its mother."

"Its MOTHER! But I'm a *boy*!"

My father laughed. "As long as it *thinks* you are its mother it will stay with you."

"All right," I said. "Then I'll *be* it."

My sister started singing, "Jamie is its mo-ther,
Jamie is its mo-ther, yah-yah-yah!"

I ignored her.

I tried to study my lessons for school. I couldn't. The baby lizard was starting to eat.

It sat on my bare knee, watching, watching. A sand fly came to take a bite out of me. It was so small that I could barely see it. The baby lizard jumped and caught it.

Chew-chew-chew, just like me, and *gulp*—just like me!—it swallowed the bug.

"Isn't that wonderful?" I shouted. "He did it all by himself!"

"He?" My mother sounded doubtful. "I think it's a little girl lizard."

"Yes," my father said. "If you had a boy lizard you could see the difference. A girl lizard is smaller, more delicate and — well, charming."

"Oh," I said. "Well! Hello, there, Izzard—my daughter, the lizard!"

Izzard was not a gecko, the kind of lizard that can see in the dark. She was an anole, a daytime lizard, so when night came she tried to hide inside my shirt. I put her in the pocket of my pajama top when I went to bed.

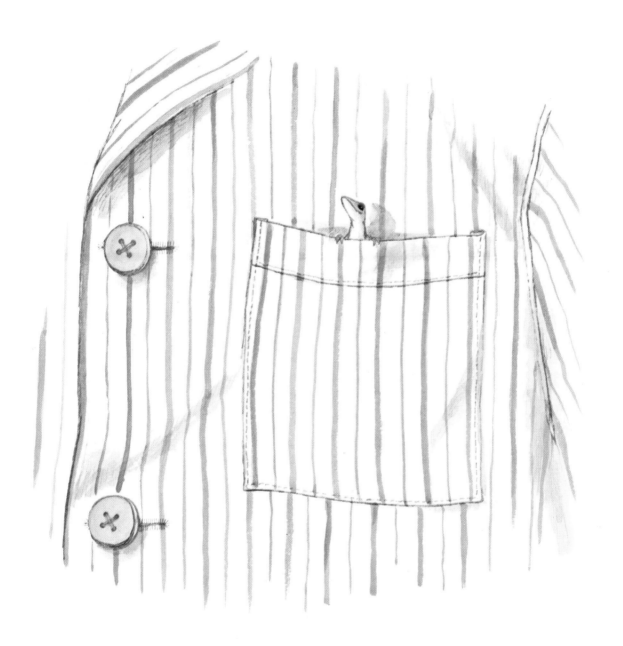

My mother worried. "You won't roll on her?"
"Oh, no!" I said. "I'll always know she's there,
even when I'm asleep."

In the morning when I woke up the sun was shining and Izzard was sitting on my cheek, looking for her breakfast. While I was still blinking my eyes she caught a sand fly and chewed and swallowed it. I noticed that regular flies were too big for her to manage, and she seemed to know it.

She stayed away from me when I took my bath because she was afraid of the water, but when I sat down to breakfast she was right there, hungry, as usual, watching for bugs.

No one told me I couldn't take her to school, so I did.

I soon wished I hadn't.

She sat on top of my head and jumped at flies.

She sat on my desk, snapping at whatever insects came by, even when they were too big for her. I think she was showing off.

The other children in the school could not pay attention to the teacher. They could only watch little Izzard and laugh.

"Jamie," the teacher said, "you will have to get rid of that lizard."

"I can't," I said. "I'm its mother."

That was the wrong thing to say, because everybody screamed and the teacher looked angry.

"Jamie, give it to me," she said. "I'll keep it in my desk until after school." She held out her hand.

Izzard hid inside my shirt.

The teacher stamped her foot. Izzard peeked out from under my chin at her.

She laughed. She couldn't help it, I could tell.

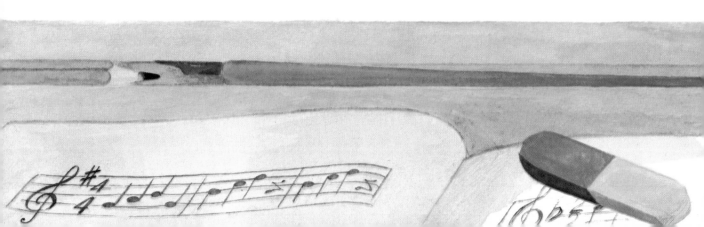

From then on I had to leave Izzard at home when I went to school or to church. She hated that, but she could not follow me because I walked too fast for her.

As soon as I came home she would run to meet me.

Izzard made a very good living eating the insects that came around me. She made such a good living that she grew very fast. Soon she was big enough to eat flies and all sorts of bugs, just like a grown-up lizzard.

One day Izzard and I saw a mongoose stalking a lizard in the yard. The lizard saw him. It had no place to hide. The house was too far away on one side, and the nearest tree was not near enough.

The lizard stood still, trying to look like a piece of wood.

The mongoose was not fooled. He crouched, ready to jump. I yelled to scare him, but it didn't work; I was too far away.

The lizard was desperate. It decided to run for the tree as I ran to help.

Too late! Pounce! went the mongoose.

Crunch-gulp. That was the end of the lizard. It was awful. I shuddered. I put my hand around Izzard. I must keep her safe.

When I played with my friends, Izzard liked to go with me. She would stay in my shirt pocket, hanging on for dear life sometimes, but always with at least one eye sticking out to keep track of what was going on.

I really hated to leave her at home where I could not protect her.

The mongoose kept sneaking around. Mongooses think lizards are delicious, and maybe they are, but I never wanted to find out.

I caught the flu. I had to stay in bed. Izzard stayed with me.

The night was hot, and Izzard slept in a crack by my bed instead of in my pajama pocket.

My mother moved me to a cooler room on the other side of the house. Izzard was asleep, and my mother was so worried about me that she forgot about her.

I was too sick to know that Izzard was not with me.

Izzard hunted and hunted and hunted for me. I know, because it took her two whole days to find me.

By that time my fever was getting better. My head was propped on a pillow, and suddenly Izzard's nose came up over the foot of my bed. Then her eyes. Then she was all there and running like mad the whole length of my bed.

I was so glad to see her that I felt better right away.

While I was getting well she stayed with me.

The more I watched her and thought about it, the more I realized that Izzard didn't know that she was a lizard. There are lizards everywhere here on St. John, in the houses and outside, but she paid no attention to any of them. She was interested only in me.

"I'll bet she thinks she's a human being, like me," I said.

"I'll bet she does," my mother agreed.

In June, while Izzard was still young, my parents took my sister and me on a long trip to New York, to visit my grandmother for the summer. Izzard was not allowed to go with me.

I worried about her. Would she forget me? Would she be able to make a living without me? Would the mongoose get her?

We came home in the fall in time for school. When we got there it was evening. Izzard was nowhere to be found. The geckos were there, the night lizards with huge eyes for seeing in the dark. They were shy, and ran from me.

I felt sad and lonely when I went to bed.

In the morning, as soon as it was light, *plop!*—there was Izzard.

She danced. She jumped. She looked into my eyes and scampered away and back again. She burrowed under my neck on the pillow and tickled me with her wriggling.

I knew she was trying to say, "I'm so *glad* to see you! Where *have* you been?"

She had been sleeping in some safe place through the night, but now she could move back into my pocket.

Her tail had a bend in it. Something *had* happened to her—I would never know what, but whew! I was happy that she was still alive and well.

The mongoose was forever hanging around outside. I kept telling Izzard never to go out there without me, but of course she could not understand.

One day when I came home from school she was nowhere in the house. It was broad daylight, so I knew she was not sleeping somewhere in hiding.

I went out the back door and looked. There she was, six feet up on a palm tree.

She started running down the tree to come to me.

At that instant I saw the mongoose, lurking under a big leaf nearby, waiting, waiting.

I yelled, "Izzard, NO!"

She couldn't understand. She came on.

The mongoose was like lightning. He pounced.

Izzard was even quicker. Terrified, she jumped straight up into the air.

She came down right on top of the mongoose's head!

Before he knew what had happened, she was off again. Jump-jump-jump—she got to me just as I was chasing the mongoose away.

She scampered up my leg and inside my shirt. She would not come out for a whole hour.

Soon after that Izzard found out she was a lizard and not a human being.

A big strong male lizard came near me to catch a bug. Izzard was jealous. She jumped at him.

Well, he gave her the worst spanking she ever had in her life.

From that moment she was different.

She stared at him, then at me.

When he left, she followed him a little way. Then she came back to look at me again.

I put out my hand to pick her up. She jumped back.

She wouldn't let me touch her!

Izzard afraid of *me*? I couldn't believe it. But she was. She wouldn't stay with me anymore. She stayed with the other lizards, sleeping with them in their secret night places, and hunting for her insect food on the walls and furniture instead of on me.

I was shocked. I was hurt.

"She's a grown-up lizard now," my father explained.

My mother said, "All of a sudden you look as big as a mountain to her. Suppose Bordeaux Mountain should reach down to pick you up. You'd be scared stiff."

"But Jamie's her *mother*!" my sister said. Once in a while a sister really understands a person better than anybody.

The next time I came home from school I thought, "By now Izzard has had time to think it over. She won't be afraid of me anymore."

I found her on the back of a chair in the living room. I went up to her—and she ran away from me!

"Oh," I moaned. "What can I do?"

"Nothing, dear," my mother said.

"If she doesn't want you," my father said, "you'll just have to forget about her."

"But how *can* he?" my sister wailed.

I couldn't and I didn't.

Summer came again, and once more we went to visit my grandmother in New York.

When we came back in the fall, as soon as we came into the house, *plop!* onto my leg came Izzard!

She ran up to my shoulder, but she couldn't see my eyes well enough from there.

She ran onto my hand and I raised her in front of my face. She stared into my eyes, first with one eye, then with the other, and wriggled. It was like old times.

My father said, "I think she missed you and decided to forgive you for not being a lizard."

"I think so too," my sister said. "You lucky thing."

"Isn't that nice?" my mother said.

Izzard had forgiven me, all right, but she didn't stay with me. She would visit me often, but she lived with the other lizards.

"She's grown-up and married now," my mother said, as if that explained everything.

Anyhow, Izzard was still my very good friend.

Guess what I found on my pillow last night when I went to bed.

A lizard egg!

Do you suppose it is Izzard's—a special present just for me?

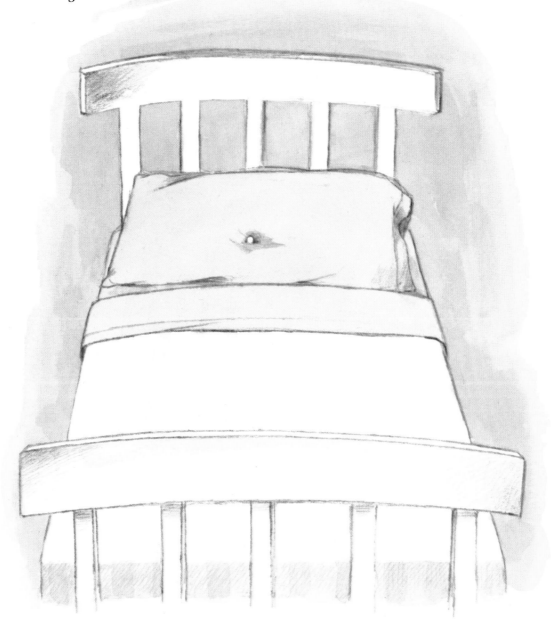